OCTICORN
PARTY!

CREATED BY

KEVIN DILLER AND JUSTIN LOWE

ILLUSTRATIONS BY

TIAN MULHOLLAND

BALZER + BRAY

An Imprint of HarperCollinsPublishers

FOR FRANKIE AND MILO, OF COURSE
—K.D.

FOR SARA, KAREN, OWEN, EVAN, MOM, AND NANA
—T.M.

Balzer + Bray is an imprint of HarperCollins Publishers.

Octicorn Party!
Text copyright © 2020 by Kevin Diller
Illustrations copyright © 2020 by Justin Lowe
All rights reserved. Manufactured in China.

ISBN 978-0-06-238794-3

20 21 22 23 24 SCP 10 9 8 7 6 5 4 3 2 1
❖
First Edition

HI, EVERYONE! I'M OCTICORN AND . . .

I AM HAVING A POOL PARTY!

OCTICORNS **LOVE** POOL PARTIES BECAUSE:
  1. THERE ARE POOLS.
  2. THEY ARE PARTIES AND . . .
  3. THERE ARE USUALLY CUPCAKES!

BUT THERE IS ONE PROBLEM.

WHAT IF NOBODY COMES?

WHAT IF I GET *SO EMBARRASSED* NO ONE COMES THAT I HAVE TO WEAR A DISGUISE FOR THE REST OF MY LIFE?

I DO *NOT* WANT TO WEAR A DISGUISE FOR THE REST OF MY LIFE BUT I ALSO *REALLY* WANT TO HAVE A POOL PARTY, SO . . .

THIS IS A VERY BIG PICKLE FOR ME!

OK. HERE I GO, I GUESS. I HOPE THIS
ISN'T A CATASTROPHE. (CATASTROPHES
ARE EVEN WORSE THAN PICKLES.)

WILL THERE BE RAINBOWS TO FLY OVER?
BECAUSE THAT'S SORT OF MY THING. IF THERE
ARE RAINBOWS TO FLY OVER, I'M IN.

UNICORN IS COMING TO MY POOL PARTY!

HI, I'M OCTI. WILL YOU COME
TO MY POOL PARTY?

I DON'T KNOW . . . I'M PRETTY SHY. CAN
IT BE A NO TALKING PARTY? WHERE WE
ALL SIT FAR AWAY FROM EACH OTHER? BY
OURSELVES? IF IT'S A NO TALKING PARTY,
I WILL COME.

TURTLE IS COMING TO MY POOL PARTY!

HI, I'M OCTI. WILL YOU COME
TO MY POOL PARTY?

UNICORN WON'T BE THERE, WILL HE? HE THINKS HE'S SO GREAT BECAUSE HE CAN FLY OVER RAINBOWS BUT HE'S A UNICORN, SO HE'S *SUPPOSED* TO BE ABLE TO FLY OVER RAINBOWS! OK, I WILL COME.

SEAHORSE IS COMING TO MY POOL PARTY!

HI, I'M OCTI. WILL YOU COME
TO MY POOL PARTY?

AS LONG AS THERE'S BREAK DANCING!
BECAUSE I LOVE BREAK DANCING! I NEED
TO LEAVE FOR THE PARTY NOW, THOUGH.
IT TAKES ME A WHILE TO GET PLACES.

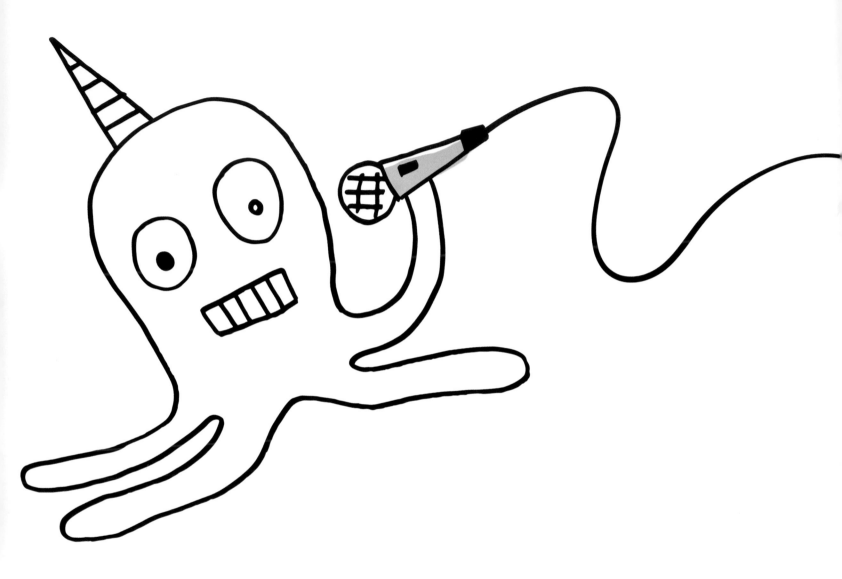

SNAIL IS COMING TO MY POOL PARTY!

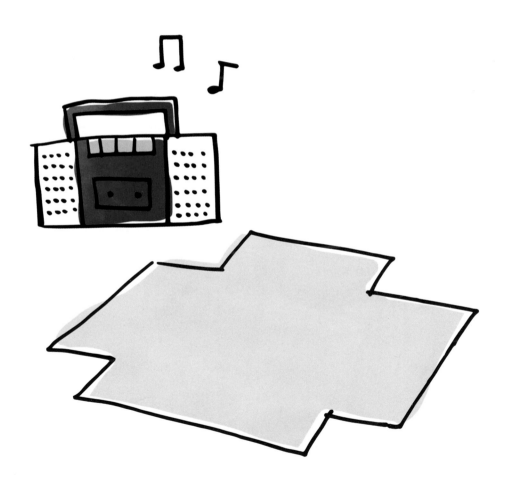

WAIT. AREN'T YOU LEAVING FOR THE PARTY?

I LEFT A MINUTE AGO. I JUST
HAVEN'T GOTTEN VERY FAR YET.

OK. GOOD LUCK!

HI, I'M OCTI. WILL YOU COME TO MY POOL PARTY?

CAN I EAT THE OTHER GUESTS?

MAYBE THIS ISN'T SUCH
A GOOD IDEA . . .

OK. FINE.

LION IS *NOT* COMING TO MY POOL PARTY!

HI, I'M OCTI. WILL YOU COME
TO MY POOL PARTY?

YOU PROBABLY KNOW WHAT
I'M GOING TO ASK. . . .

YES, THERE CAN BE
WOOD TO CHUCK.

FANTASTIC! I WILL BE THERE!

THIS IS THE **BEST DAY OF MY LIFE!** I AM HAVING A FLY OVER RAINBOWS, NO TALKING, UNICORN IS NOT INVITED, BREAK DANCING, WOOD CHUCKING, GUESTS MAY *NOT* EAT OTHER GUESTS, CUPCAKE POOL PARTY!

WAIT.

WHAT WAS I THINKING?!

UNICORN *IS* INVITED, SO SEAHORSE WILL HAVE A BAD TIME, SNAILS ARE *TERRIFIED* OF WOOD CHUCKING, UNICORN WILL TALK TURTLE RIGHT BACK INTO HIS SHELL, AND LION WILL PROBABLY SHOW UP AND TRY TO EAT THE OTHER GUESTS!

THIS IS A CATASTROPHE!

OH, WELL. I GUESS I'M NOT
HAVING THAT PARTY AFTER ALL.

I AM HAVING A DO WHAT YOU WANT, BE WHO YOU ARE, NO MATTER WHAT ANYONE ELSE THINKS, PARTY INSTEAD!

PARTY HATS FOR EVERYONE!

SORRY, LION, YOU HAVE TO STAY OUTSIDE. BUT YOU *CAN* HAVE A CUPCAKE.